Lucy fell down the Mountain

by Kevin Cornell

Farrar Straus Giroux
NEW YORK

FOR KIM,
WHO HOLDS MY HAND

Farrar Straus Giroux Books for Young Readers
An imprint of Macmillan Publishing Group, LLC
175 Fifth Avenue, New York, NY 10010

COLOR SEPARATIONS BY: Bright Arts (H.K.) Ltd.

PRINTED IN: China

by RR Donnelley Asia Printing Solutions Ltd.,
Dongguan City, Guangdong Province

EDITED by GRACE KENDALL

DESIGNED by ANNE DIEBEL

FIRST EDITION, 2018

1 3 5 7 9 10 8 6 4 2

mackids.com

LIBRARY of CONGRESS CONTROL NUMBER: 2018932019
ISBN: 978-0-374-30608-3

OUR BOOKS MAY BE PURCHASED
IN BULK FOR PROMOTIONAL, EDUCATIONAL,
OR BUSINESS USE. PLEASE CONTACT YOUR LOCAL
BOOKSELLER OR THE MACMILLAN CORPORATE
AND PREMIUM SALES DEPARTMENT AT
(800) 221-7945 ext. 5442 OR BY E-MAIL AT
MACMILLANSPECIALMARKETS@MACMILLAN.COM.

Lucy fell down the mountain.

She bumped her head on the ROCKS.

And
snow stuck
to her
BUTT.

Faster
and
faster
she
fell...

...until she
came upon
a mountain
man.

"Great idea,
little girl!" said the
mountain man.

"Noooo!"
cried lucy.
"I meant toss
it to ME!!"

"oh,"
said the
mountain man.
"That would
have made more
sense."

Lucy's distant reply was too hard to hear...

which is probably for the best.

Down, down, down
the mountain,
Lucy fell.

When beside
her appeared ...
a bungeeing duck!

"What luck!" exclaimed Lucy.

"I can bounce back up with you!"

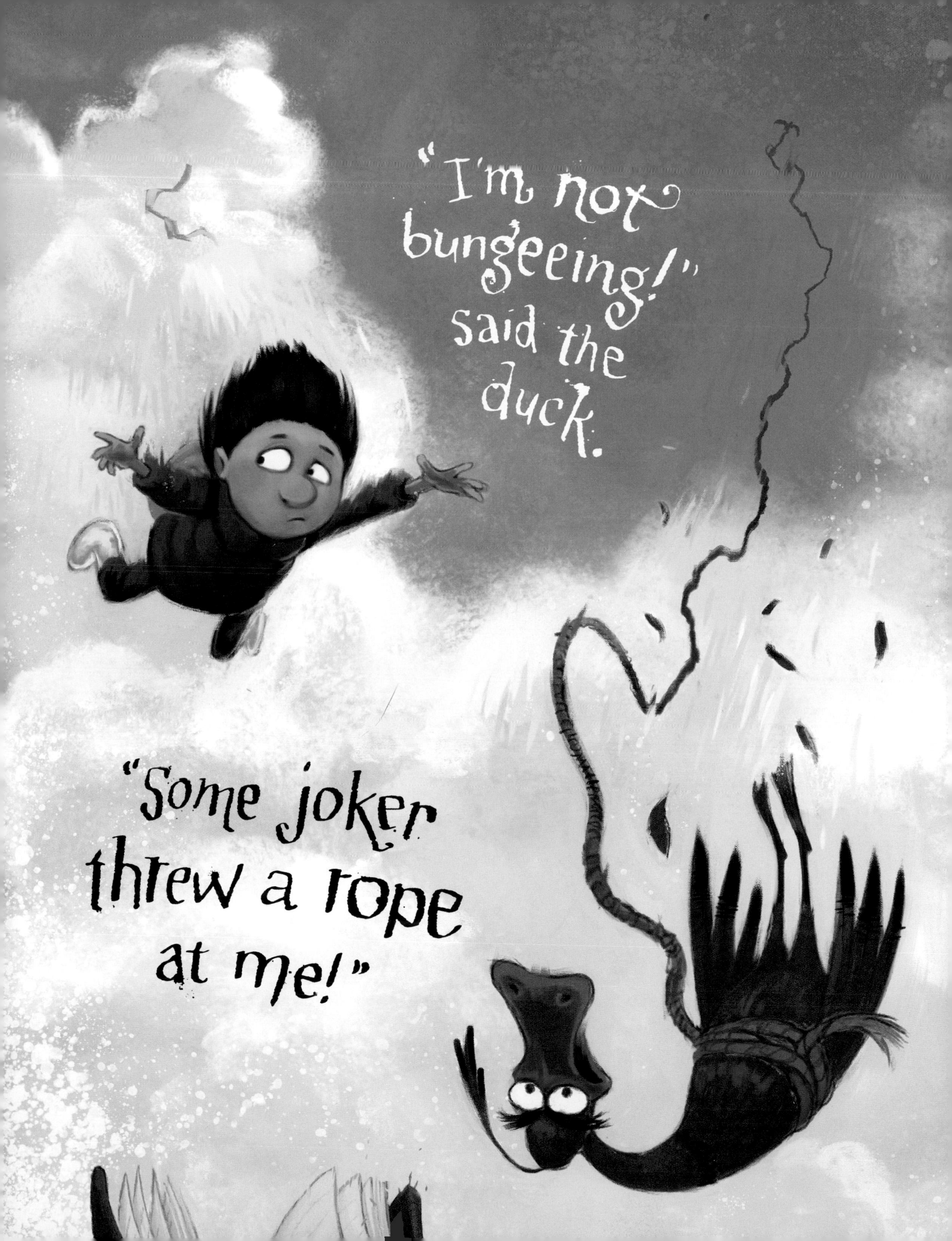

"I'm not bungeeing!" said the duck.

"Some joker threw a rope at me!"

Fortunately, Lucy fell into a cave hole...

...before needing to explain.

The cave hole
was dry and warm.
It was perfect!

Except for...

"Ahhh!"
shrieked the
bear pile,
shuffling...

"How did you
get in our
cave hole!?"

"I fell in,"
said Lucy.

"Well, fall back out!" said the bear pile.

"Can't I stay?" asked Lucy. "My head hurts, my butt is freezing..."

...and falling down a mountain has been really terrifying."

The bear pile put
their arms around
Lucy gently.

In her ear she felt a
tickle, as a single bear
whispered,

"When bears
feel like that...

Lucy
wished...

she had
a pile.

So she
piled her
legs on her
chest...

and her
head on her
knees...

...and lucy fell down the mountain until she wasn't falling anymore.

Down the mountain Lucy zoomed like a tiny kid comet,

gathering globs of sticky white snow!

Faster and faster the pile rolled!

So fast, in fact, she was catching up...

...to two **distant dots**... ...tumbling from the **SKY!**

BOOM! went the mountain man, grabbing the end!

Slower and slower and slower they rolled...

like the rope was an anchor and their pile a boat...

Until the great snowy pile reached the end of the slope...

...and rested gently beside the Handsome Chalet.

cocoa

No harm, done!

"Well...

...no harm a nice cup of cocoa couldn't fix.